Mary, Mary, quite contrary,
how does your garden grow?
With silver bells
and cockleshells
and pretty maids all in a row.

For Suzanne: every garden should have such a splendid bloom—A. McQ.

To Ethan and Frankie with love—R. B.

First paperback edition 2017
2014 First US Edition
Text copyright © 2014 by Anna McQuinn
Illustrations copyright © 2014 by Rosalind Beardshaw

Published by Charlesbridge
85 Main Street
Watertown, MA 02472
(617) 926-0329
www.charlesbridge.com

First published in the United Kingdom in 2014 by Alanna Books, 46 Chalvey Road East, Slough,
Berkshire, SL1 2LR, United Kingdom, as *Lulu Loves Flowers*. Copyright © 2014 Alanna Books
www.alannabooks.com

Library of Congress Cataloging-in-Publication Data
McQuinn, Anna, author.
    Lola plants a garden/Anna McQuinn; illustrated by Rosalind Beardshaw.
        pages cm
    Summary: Lola plants a flower garden with her parents' help, and watches it grow.
    ISBN 978-1-58089-694-8 (reinforced for library use)
    ISBN 978-1-58089-695-5 (softcover)
    ISBN 978-1-60734-745-3 (ebook)
    ISBN 978-1-60734-697-5 (ebook pdf)
1. Flower gardening—Juvenile fiction. 2. African American girls—Juvenile fiction.
3. African American families—Juvenile fiction. [1. Flower gardening—Fiction.
2. Gardening—Fiction. 3. African Americans—Fiction. 4. Family life—Fiction.]
I. Beardshaw, Rosalind, illustrator. II. Title.
PZ7.M47883Lr 2014
[E]—dc23   2013022072

Printed in China
(hc) 10 9 8 7
(sc) 10 9 8 7 6

Illustrations done in acrylic on paper
Display type set in Garamouche Bold
Text type set in Billy by SparkyType
Color separations by KHL Chroma Graphics, Singapore
Printed by 1010 Printing International Limited in Huizhou, Guangdong, China
Production supervision by Brian G. Walker
Designed by Martha MacLeod Sikkema and Sarah Richards Taylor

Lola Plants a Garden

Anna McQuinn
Illustrated by Rosalind Beardshaw

ﯫ Charlesbridge

Lola loves her book of garden poems.
Her favorite poem
is the one about Mary Mary.

Lola wants to plant a garden.
Mommy says there is room
near the vegetables.

Lola gets books about gardens
from the library.

She chooses her favorite flowers
from the books.

Mommy makes a list.

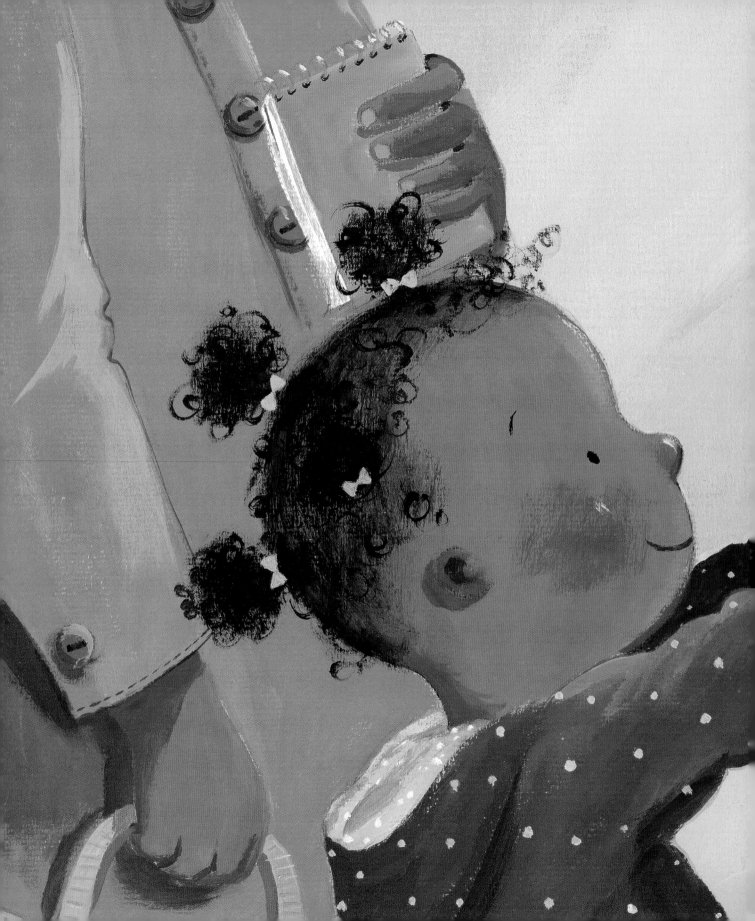

They go to the
garden store to buy seeds.

Lola and Mommy make the garden.

The seed packets mark
where the flowers are planted.

Lola will have to wait
a long time for them to grow.

Lola makes her own flower book
while she waits.

Mommy types the Mary Mary poem, and Lola glues it in.

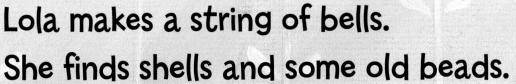

Lola makes a string of bells.
She finds shells and some old beads.

She even makes
a little Mary Mary.

One day Lola sees tiny green shoots!

She pulls up weeds
so the shoots can grow.

Lola's flowers grow bigger.
They open up to the sun.

Daddy helps Lola
hang her shiny bells.

Lola finds Mary Mary a special spot.
It's just perfect.

Orla, Ben, and Ty are coming
to see Lola's garden.
Lola and Mommy make cupcakes.

Lola wears her flower shirt.
Mommy helps Lola with her hair.

Lola's friends love everything about her garden.

They share the crunchy peas
and sweet strawberries
that Mommy grew.

Then Lola makes up a story about Mary Mary.

What kind of garden will Lola plant next?

Lola, Lola, extraordinary,
how does your garden grow?
With flower seeds
and shells and beads
and happy friends all in a row.